# ED MOUSE
## FINDS OUT ABOUT
## DIRECTION

Belitha Press

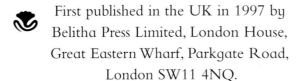First published in the UK in 1997 by
Belitha Press Limited, London House,
Great Eastern Wharf, Parkgate Road,
London SW11 4NQ.

ISBN 1 85561 722 6

British Library in Cataloguing in Publication Data for this book
is available from the British Library.

Printed in Hong Kong

Series Editor: Honor Head
Series Designer: Helen James
Illustrator: Adam Stower/Wildlife Art Agency
Consultants: Wendy Body and Chris Powling

# ED MOUSE
## FINDS OUT ABOUT

**DIRECTION**

## Illustrated by Adam Stower

Meet Ed Mouse. He lives in a mousehole in the kitchen of a big house. Ed Mouse has lots of adventures...why don't you join him?

Hi there! I'm Ed.

5

Ed Mouse is very excited. Today he's going to his friend Jo's birthday party. He's wrapped her present in bright yellow paper and put it under the table in a bag.

Where is Ed? Where
is the spider? Where
are the buttons?

Ed's nearly ready to go but he's lost his special blue glove. He looks in the box which is on the table next to the mug.

Ed has found his blue glove. Now he looks for Jo's card. It isn't next to the books on the top shelf and it isn't on the bottom shelf.

*What is next to the books on the top shelf? What is under the bottom shelf?*

Ed has found Jo's card. It was on the middle shelf. He sits down to write the card. He uses his right paw.

13

Ed is now ready to
go to Jo's party. He
puts on his gloves.
He wears the blue
glove on his left paw
and the red glove on
his right paw.

Ed rushes across the floor towards the door. He's in such a hurry that he trips over the wastepaper bin. Luckily he doesn't hurt himself.

Oops!

What else is rushing
across the floor?
Which side of the door
is Ed's red bike?

17

Outside in the big kitchen Ed sees Jo on top of the kitchen table. She tells Ed to hurry up because the party has started.

18

*Where are the shoes? What is outside the mousehole?*

19

Ed climbs up. Jo's other friends are already there. Tom is behind a glass making a funny face. Pip is sliding down a banana.

Happy birthday!

Whee!

Who is on top of the table? What is behind the glasses?

21

The friends play hide-and-seek. Ed stands in front of the vase and covers his eyes. Jo, Pip and Tom hide. Then Ed has to find them.

Which paw is Ed using to cover his eyes? What is in front of the cake?

23

Jo hides inside the
sugar bowl. Ed finds
her and tips her out.
He tips out all the
sugar, too. He soon
finds Pip and Tom
as well.

What is inside the big brown bowl? Who is hiding inside the mug?

25

Tom wants to have a jumping race. The friends have to jump over the cheese and straws. Ed is hungry and would rather eat the cheese.

Jo opens her present. It is a teddy bear just like Ed's. Now it's time to go home. Ed slides slowly back down the tablecloth. Bye-bye Ed.

Thanks for the present.

# Notes for parents and teachers

This book is about the words used to describe direction and the position of things. Read the story through so that the children become familiar with the story and the characters. Point out the speech bubbles and make sure that the children understand that these show someone talking.

Once the children are familiar with the story, read it through again and ask them to answer the boxed questions. If the speech bubbles contain questions, discuss these. On pages 8-9 and 10-11, encourage the children to look for the missing objects.

Ask the children to describe in their own words what happens in the story using the directional words from the story.

**Show Ed the way**
In a familiar setting such as the classroom or home, ask the children to describe how Ed would get from one spot to another, eg, from the bookshelf to the door.

**Hide-and-seek**
Arrange a collection of containers, such as mugs, tins or a toy handbag on a table or on the floor. Hide a prize such as a toy or sweet in one of the containers. Let the children take it in turns to find the prize by asking a question such as, 'Is it in the tin behind the bag?' The one who finds the prize keeps it and hides the next prize.

## Left and right

Ask the children to pretend to do different actions such as waving using the left or right side of their bodies. For those who find this difficult, put a yellow sticky note on their right foot or tie a piece of coloured wool around one wrist.

## Make Ed Mouse gloves

Make a pair of gloves like Ed Mouse's using pieces of felt or thick blue and red paper. Trace around the children's fingers and thumb and then cut out the shape twice for each hand. Sew the two halves of each glove together.

*Children do not always choose to use only their left or right hand for a long time, and the age at which they do choose varies. Do not push them to choose one or the other if they are not ready to do so.*

## Talk about party food

Look at the pictures of Jo's party. Talk about the food the children can see. Ask them which food or drink they would choose for a party and why. Ask them to draw their favourite foods.

## Send a message

Discuss with the children what they would write in a birthday card or Christmas card. Go on to talk about what they would write in a letter to a friend or family member. Ask them to make a greetings card and write a message in it.

# List of words

| | |
|---|---|
| **across** | Ed rushes across the floor. |
| **behind** | Tom is behind the glass. |
| **bottom** | The dinosaur is on the bottom shelf. |
| **down** | Pip is sliding down the banana. |
| **in** | Jo's present is in a big bag. |
| **in front** | Ed stands in front of the vase. |
| **inside** | Jo hides inside the sugar bowl. |
| **left** | Ed wears his blue glove on his left paw. |
| **middle** | The card is on the middle shelf. |
| **next to** | The box is next to the robot. |
| **on** | The box is on the table. |
| **on top** | Jo is on top of the table. |
| **outside** | Ed is outside his mousehole. |
| **over** | Tom jumps over the cheese and straws. |
| **right** | Ed wears his red glove on his right paw. |
| **towards** | Ed is going towards the door. |
| **under** | Jo's birthday present is under the table. |
| **up** | Ed climbs up to the party. |